First Published in Great Britain in 2008
by W.F Graham (Northampton) Ltd
for Lomond Books Ltd, Broxburn, EH52 5NF

© Lomond Books Ltd 2008

ISBN 1-842-04122-2

A long time ago before even your Granny and Grandad were born, a Skye Terrier lived in a churchyard in Edinburgh. The Terrier's name was Bobby and the churchyard was called Greyfriars, so everybody called him Greyfriars Bobby.

Bobby had a friend, a black cat called Frankie, and Bobby and Frankie had adventures around Edinburgh.

They would go down to Princes Street to see all the hustle and bustle of the people going to the big shops.

Frankie and Bobby enjoyed nothing more than dodging between the horses and carts!

They would go down the Royal Mile to Holyrood Palace and Holyrood Park where they would chase swans!

They would go to the market when the farmers came to Edinburgh with their cows and their sheep. Bobby and Frankie would help the farmers round them up.

Everybody knew Bobby and Frankie and would say "Hello Bobby", "hello Frankie!" when they saw them. In reply, Bobby would bark and Frankie would miaow.

One day there was a commotion on the Royal Mile and Bobby and Frankie went to see what was going on.

Angus, the Highland soldier, had run into a horse and was sitting by the road feeling dizzy!

"Hello Bobby, hello Frankie!", groaned Angus. "I've hurt myself and I have to be at the castle in ten minutes! Bobby, I need your help! Can you help me, Bob?" he asked. Bobby looked at Frankie and looked back at Angus and gave a bark and wagged his tail.

"Thanks Bobby! Thanks Frankie!" said Angus, "Everyday at one o'clock a gun is fired at Edinburgh Castle so that people know it is one o'clock, and it is my job to make sure that it is fired exactly on time. Now it's up to you and there is no time to waste!"

Bobby gave a bark and Frankie gave a miaow and off they went. Up the Royal Mile, past the houses and the shops, past St. Giles Cathedral. Past the horses and carts. They ran fast as they could with Bobby leading the way as they raced into the castle!

You could see all of Edinburgh from the castle, but Bobby and Frankie had no time to enjoy the view!

There were only seconds to go and the gun was in sight! With a great leap, Bobby jumped past all the visitors and the soldiers and fired the gun!

The gun went BOOM! The tourists and soldiers cheered and all the people of Edinburgh looked at their watches. It was one o'clock. Bobby had done it!

Bobby and Frankie had many more adventures. Bobby became the most famous dog in Scotland. A statue of Bobby was built near his home at Greyfriars churchyard.

Today, visitors from all over the world come to Edinburgh to see the castle, hear the one o'clock gun and visit the statue of Greyfrairs Bobby, the little dog who saved the day!